the new batch

CUPCAKE DIARIES

Natalie's Sprinkle of light

By Coco Simon
author of Cupcake Diaries

Illustrated by Manuela lópez

Simon Spotlight
New York   Amsterdam/Antwerp   london
Toronto   Sydney/Melbourne   New Delhi

SIMON SPOTLIGHT

An imprint of Simon & Schuster Children's Publishing Division

1230 Avenue of the Americas, New York, New York 10020

This Simon Spotlight hardcover edition August 2025

© 2025 by Simon & Schuster, LLC

Also available in a Simon Spotlight paperback edition.

For information about special discounts for bulk purchases, please contact Simon & Schuster Special Sales at 1-866-506-1949 or business@simonandschuster.com.

Simon & Schuster strongly believes in freedom of expression and stands against censorship in all its forms. For more information, visit BooksBelong.com.

The Simon & Schuster Speakers Bureau can bring authors to your live event. For more information or to book an event, contact the Simon & Schuster Speakers Bureau at 1-866-248-3049 or visit our website at www.simonspeakers.com.

Text by Tracy West • Illustrations by Manuela López • Book design by Brittany Fetcho

The illustrations for this book were rendered digitally.

The text of this book was set in Cardo.

Manufactured in the United States of America 0725 LAK

2 4 6 8 10 9 7 5 3 1

Library of Congress Cataloging-in-Publication Data

Names: Simon, Coco, author. | López, Manuela, 1985– illustrator. | Simon, Coco. Cupcake diaries, the new batch ; 6. Title: Natalie's sprinkle of light! / by Coco Simon ; illustrated by Manuela López.

Description: New York : Simon Spotlight, 2025. | Series: Cupcake diaries, the new batch ; 6 | Audience term: Children | Summary: Natalie's cupcake club friends help her navigate a jealous bully.

Identifiers: LCCN 2024040314 (print) | LCCN 2024040315 (ebook) | ISBN 9781665980388 (paperback) | ISBN 9781665980395 (hardcover) | ISBN 9781665980401 (ebook)

Subjects: LCSH: Baking—Juvenile fiction. | Jealousy—Juvenile fiction. | Bullying—Juvenile fiction. | Friendship—Juvenile fiction. | CYAC: Baking—Fiction. | Jealousy—Fiction. | Bullies and bullying—Fiction. | Friendship—Fiction. Classification: LCC PZ7.S60357 Nb 2025 (print) | LCC PZ7.S60357 (ebook) | DDC [Fic]—dc23/eng/20250204

LC record available at https://lccn.loc.gov/2024040314

LC ebook record available at https://lccn.loc.gov/2024040315

CONTENTS

Chapter 1

The Countdown

"I can always tell when it's about to rain," I said, turning to Emily.

"Really? That's very impressive," she replied.

"Yeah, the clouds give it away. Also, my tablet showed me the weather this morning." I flashed my tablet at Emily and smiled. "See? Tuesday, rainy."

"Makes sense." Emily chuckled as

she slid into the bus seat next to me and carefully started organizing the contents of her book bag.

"I can't believe your birthday is coming up in a few weeks!" I enthusiastically shouted to Emily.

"I know! I can't wait!" Emily exclaimed as she straightened up and pulled a piece of lint off her shirt. "And yours is next! Are you excited?" she continued.

"Definitely. I'm counting down the days!" I replied.

"Amazing!" Emily said. "I always count down important dates too. Want to see?"

I gave her a smile. Emily knows that she can be herself around me. She pulled out her planner and showed me her perfectly neat calendar with stickies, highlighted words, and to-do lists. "Are you doing anything special for your birthday?" she asked.

"Well!" I snapped my fingers together. "I'm so glad you asked! My parents had a friend from Brazil over the other night, and they brought the most delicious chocolate treat ever! It was like a party for my taste buds. Wanna guess what it was? I'll give you a hint. Not cupcakes," I nudged playfully.

"Hmm. Chocolate treat. Not cupcakes. Double chocolate chip cookies?" Emily guessed.

"Nope, but now I'm craving them! Okay, okay, I'll tell you . . . they're called *brigadeiros*," I said, trying to use my best Portuguese accent.

"Brigadeiros!" Emily repeated. "Oh wow, I've never heard of them. What are they? What do they taste like?" Em leaned in closer to listen.

"It's a chocolate dessert that's popular in Brazil. It's like a truffle. They're always at birthday parties in Brazil!" I told her.

"That sounds so good—and, like, the perfect birthday treat!" Emily smiled.

"Yep, and the best part is that they don't require too many ingredients. You just need condensed milk, unsalted butter, cocoa powder, and chocolate sprinkles!" I said gleefully.

"*Brigadeiros* sound delicious!" Em said as the bus stopped and we walked off together.

Just thinking about *brigadeiros* had me hungry for some, but now was not the time to think about soft, delicious, out-of-this-world desserts. I had to get to homeroom and read over the lyrics to my big solo in chorus that I'm practicing in class later today!

Chapter 2

A Sour Solo

I ended up arriving to chorus class a little late. When I walked in everyone was standing in position, ready to practice our group song. I'd just gotten a little distracted in the halls thinking about Emily's birthday and my own.

Ms. Geradi is one of the nicest teachers I have; she always encourages us to just have fun and do our best. I love being in chorus, and not just because I was one of two students picked to sing a solo for the class final project this Friday. The other solo went to my classmate Matthew, who was also in the theater club with me.

When Ms. Geradi called me to the front of the room, I heard Helena, who is not my friend, say to her friends as I passed by, "I bet Natalie only got the solo because she's so loud and everyone knows she's in the Mini Cupcake Club. She's such a suck-up!"

Normally that stuff doesn't bother me, but I was really excited to sing my solo, and I'd earned it. I practiced every day and even watched singing tutorials to brush up on some notes that I found difficult.

I forced out a smile and started to sing my solo. Ms. Geradi smiled back.

"See? Such a suck-up. Her voice isn't even that good, just like her cupcakes," Helena whispered loudly in a menacing tone.

I was always taught that sometimes bullies like Helena may be going through something that makes them act out and be mean, so I decided not to say anything and just smile at her instead. Besides, I would rather focus on the positive things in my life, and I have friends who support me. Plus, I know I didn't get this solo because of the Mini Cupcake Club, even though our cupcakes are delicious. I got it because I have a great voice!

When I got to lunch the next period, I couldn't help but bring up Helena. It was still bothering me, and what are friends for if not to vent?

"I just can't believe she thinks I got the solo just because I'm in the Mini Cupcake Club," I said to my friends, shaking my head and staring down at my sandwich.

"I'm sorry, Natalie. Maybe she was having a bad day," Emily offered.

"Yeah, remember, even if other people are unkind, it's best we choose kindness," Ren added softly.

I know we just celebrated Kindness Week at school, but why do I have to be kind to a bully? I thought.

"Other than Helena being mean, how was chorus? Did you get to practice your solo?" Alana asked. She could tell I was a little annoyed.

"Fine," I said, grabbing my tray and leaving the lunch table. I didn't want my friends to see how upset I was.

For the rest of the day, I couldn't stop thinking about how things had gone at lunch, so I decided I should call my friends later that night. We all got on a video chat on our tablets, and I told them I was sorry for leaving without saying goodbye.

"I just felt disappointed, like none of you were supporting me when I came to you with a problem," I admitted.

Ren jumped in first. "It's okay, Natalie. We totally understand. And I'm sorry." Everyone nodded in agreement and sent little heart emojis through the screen.

"Thank you for opening up and being honest," Ethan said.

Then my friends reminded me of what a great singer I am and how much I deserved to sing the solo. I could feel my confidence coming back.

Suddenly, Alana said she had to jump off the call, but she didn't explain why. The rest of us left the call soon after that. I felt better telling my friends how I felt.

Chapter 3

Big Bully Business

The next day, I felt a little better going to chorus after being assured that my friends do support me and think I'm a talented singer. *I can do anything,* I coached myself as I walked through the doors.

"Look who it is!" Helena immediately taunted me. "Hey, Natalie, I'm sorry I said you shouldn't sing *solo.* I meant to say you should sing SO LOW, so no one can hear you!" She turned to her friends and laughed.

I tried to ignore her, but she was really getting into my head. For the rest of class, we practiced our group songs. I sang quietly for maybe the first time ever. I thought I could keep my head down till the bell rang, but then Ms. Geradi made an announcement.

"Okay, class, can our two solo singers come up to the front to practice the final project, please?"

Oh no, I thought.

As Matthew and I walked past Helena and her friends, I heard her whisper to them, "You know Natalie is an identical twin, right? Maybe that's why she has only half a voice." Helena snickered, and her friends started to laugh with her.

When I got to the front of the classroom, I took a deep breath and tried to shake it off.

My part was first.

I began to sing, but then I started to forget the lyrics. I knew this song by heart. Everyone does, even my parents! Plus, I'm the one who's always telling Emily to be more confident. I couldn't let Helena make me less confident. I let out a sigh.

"Don't worry, Natalie. Everyone makes mistakes," Ms. Geradi said soothingly. "Mistakes don't define us. Let's try again tomorrow, okay? Matthew, are you ready?"

"Thanks, Ms. Geradi," I mumbled as I walked back to my seat.

"Teacher's pet," Helena scoffed.

When it was lunchtime, I walked slowly to the cafeteria. My mind had been full of doubts all morning. *What if I'm not a good singer? Does everyone think that? Am I really a teacher's pet? Is Ms. Geradi just being nice to me because she's nice?*

"Hey, Natalie, where have you been?" Emily asked when I finally arrived at our lunch table. "We were just talking about a new last-minute order Alana got last night."

"Oh, really?" I said, avoiding her question. "What order? From who?" I tried sounding cheerful.

"Helena's parents emailed me last night asking for mini cupcakes for her birthday party on Saturday. That's why I had to get off the call. I couldn't believe it!" Alana said.

"Why? It's not like it's our first time getting an email request," I said. Then I realized all my friends were looking at me strangely. The name finally registered. "Wait. Did you say *Helena's* parents?"

Alana nodded.

"Absolutely not! Her parents can just get store-bought cupcakes!" I said firmly.

"I know she's not the nicest, but it would be really bad for business to turn down an order that would help our growth," Alana replied.

I'm sure Alana had already crunched the numbers. Alana is great at math, just like my twin sister, Stephanie. *It probably would be bad to not take the request,* I thought.

"Maybe we should talk to Helena and bring everything out in the open. Remember, kindness first!" Ren suggested.

I grunted and followed my friends over to Helena's table.

"Hey, Helena, can we talk for a minute?" I began.

Helena dropped her sandwich and looked at me. "Oh, it's you."

"Yeah, it's me. And my friends, Emily, Alana—"

"I know who they are," Helena interrupted. "How may I help you, Natalie?"

"I just wanted to ask why you're saying all those things about me in chorus," I said in a steady voice.

"Whatever do you mean?" Helena fluttered her eyelashes at me.

"When you said those things about my singing," I continued more quietly.

"I think you misunderstood, Natalie."
Helena smiled. "I simply said you had
a *beauuutiful* voice that matched your
beauuutiful cupcakes." Helena looked at her
friends, and they all turned to us wearing
that same fake smile on Helena's face.

I looked at my friends and could tell they weren't buying whatever she was selling. Suddenly, I started to feel really awkward. I looked at Helena again.

"All right . . . well, good talk," I said, turning around to leave.

"I guess that didn't really go well," Alana said as we left.

I nodded. I didn't know what to do about that cupcake order. Could we really bake cupcakes for Helena's birthday?

Chapter 4

Friends Make Life Sweeter

The next day when I got home from school, I sat in the kitchen and waited for my friends to arrive. I looked around wondering how this talk about Helena was going to go. That's when I noticed a note from my twin sister, Stephanie, on the refrigerator.

THERE ARE TWO BRIGADEIROS LEFT, ONE FOR YOU AND ONE FOR ME, TWINSIE!

That was the best news I'd gotten all day.

Soon my friends arrived one by one.

"Did you see Helena at school today?" Ren asked.

"Yep," I said as I bit my lower lip.

"That bad, huh?" Alana replied.

I nodded. "Yeah, and I think it's gotten worse since we tried to talk to her yesterday. I don't know what her problem is with me!"

"It's like I always say, let the art talk," Ethan piped up.

"When have you ever said that, Ethan?" I said with a laugh.

"Just now, weren't you listening?" he replied. "Plus, I have a great idea for these birthday party cupcakes. Picture this: cereal, milk, and salami." Ethan looked toward the sky as if he were imagining his cupcakes on a billboard sign or something.

"Eww!" The rest of the club all groaned practically at the same time.

"Hey now, I'm open to ideas, but I have to say, that is the combination Helena deserves," Ethan said, plopping himself onto a chair.

I sighed. Ren jumped in to avoid an awkward silence. "Listen, Natalie. We're all really sorry things have gotten worse with Helena."

"Trust me, Nat. You're amazing, and maybe Helena is just jealous," Ethan said.

"Yeah!" my friends agreed.

Just then my sister walked in. Stephanie noticed all our serious faces. "Whoa, what did I walk into? Deep conversation time?"

"Natalie's getting bullied," Alana replied quickly.

"Oh no, I'm so sorry. Who's bullying you?" asked Stephanie.

"Helena," I told her.

"Hmm . . . I don't think I know her, but what I do know is how horrible that feels. Remember when people used to bully us for being twins?"

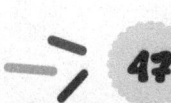

"Yeah, but that was different. We were together. Now I'm just being teased by myself." I placed my elbows on the counter and plopped my face into my hands. I was a little embarrassed to reveal how much this was bothering me.

"You're right, Natalie. It is different," Stephanie said, coming over to give me a hug. "Let us know what we can do to help."

It felt good having a real face-to-face conversation with people who cared about me, focusing on what was really important: friendship and our mini cupcake club.

Chapter Five

Olá, Brigadeiros!

As our conversation about Helena ended, Emily reminded me about the cupcake idea I'd had.

"Do you want to tell everyone, or should I?" she asked, pushing a strand of hair off her face.

"Ooh, I love new cupcake ideas. What is it? Green slime cupcakes that smell like onions?" Ethan teased.

"Um, not quite," I said with a chuckle.

"I was telling Emily about *brigadeiros*." Before I could explain, Stephanie had already looked them up on her tablet and was showing everyone.

"Oh, wow, they look tasty!" Ren gasped.

"So, would the whole cupcake be like this?" Ethan wondered. "Maybe it could use a little cheese? . . . I'm joking!"

"Hmm, I haven't gotten that far yet," I answered.

"Sooo . . . does this mean we're going to accept Helena's birthday party order?" Ren said, smiling.

"Well?" Alana put her arm around my shoulder.

"As our marketing agent . . . ," I began, "I have to look at all the variables . . . and I think it is in our best interest to say . . . yes. Helena still needs to apologize to me, but in the meantime, we can start working on this batch of cupcakes."

"I agree," said Stephanie. "And I also agree that cupcakes based on *brigadeiros* is a great idea. Nice going, sis."

"But wait, we still don't know what they taste like," Ethan said, eyeing the sticky note on the refrigerator.

"Go ahead," my sister said with a grin.

I got the last two *brigadeiros* out of the refrigerator and cut them into small pieces so everyone could have a taste.

"Woooow!" Ethan said, savoring the bite in his mouth.

"Yep, my feelings exactly!" Alana agreed.

"They seriously melt in your mouth." Ren sounded shocked and amazed at the same time.

"These are delicious," Emily exclaimed. "Even better than I imagined."

"You know what would be great with this? Ketchup," Ethan joked.

"ETHAN!" We all laughed.

I was happy that we decided as a group to keep going and not let someone in a permanent bad mood ruin our club and our business.

Chapter 6

A Solo Role of a Lifetime

On Friday, I walked into chorus with my head held high. I felt confident about my solo again and wasn't going to let anyone make me feel bad about it. Nope. Nothing could go wrong. No more bad news for me, ever.

"Hi, class, I'm afraid I have some bad news," Ms. Geradi said once everyone had settled down.

Are you kidding me? I thought.

"Matthew is out sick, so he won't be able to sing his solo for the group song we're singing as the class final project."

I looked around and saw my classmates chatting among themselves. I took a deep breath and raised my hand.

"Ms. Geradi, do you think it would be okay if Helena sings the solo? I mean, only if you want to, Helena," I suggested, smiling.

Ms. Geradi pushed up her glasses and tapped her chin. "Hmm . . . that's not a bad idea at all, Natalie. Would that be something you'd be open to, Helena?" Ms. Geradi asked kindly.

I looked over at Helena. Her face turned bright red and then she replied softly. "Well . . . I did memorize that section, just in case I got the part . . . yeah, yeah, I could do it," she said, standing up taller.

"Well, there we have it, folks. The show will go on!" Ms. Geradi cheered.

"What show? I thought this was just practice," a kid in the back asked, confused.

I turned to Helena and smiled. She smiled back at me.

When it was her turn, Helena sang beautifully. And I'm happy to report that we performed our final assignment wonderfully.

Maybe Ren was right: kindness first.

Chapter 7

Stop, Bake, and Roll

Friday after school, everyone came over to my place to start baking the *brigadeiro* cupcakes. I wasn't exactly sure of the details yet, but I knew I wanted the same flavors.

"Okay, Ethan, *serious* question—no stinky, smelly, or sticky answers," I said, smiling and tilting my head.

"You got it, coach. Whatcha need?"

Ethan responded. He smiled back at me.

"Do you think we should make the whole cupcake a *brigadeiro* or just base our recipe on them?" I asked him.

"Well, that is a very serious question. Maybe—and I'm just spitballin' here—we stick with the *brigadeiro* theme for either the cupcake *or* the frosting. That way, it's still an original creation by our club."

Ethan may have really off-the-wall ideas sometimes, but he's also really clever and knows just what to say when it counts.

"That's interesting. If we make just the cupcake portion a *brigadeiro* . . . ," Ren started.

"But do you think it will be too heavy?" Emily gently broke in. I remember her examining every inch of the *brigadeiro* yesterday, its fudgy consistency inside.

"Valid point, valid point," Ethan said. "Wait, I got it. Let's use the *brigadeiro* ingredients for the frosting and—"

"And then use vanilla batter for the cake part, with sprinkles on top, like confetti cupcakes!" Alana finished for him.

"Rainbow sprinkles!" Ren hopped on to the idea train. "Staying close to the traditional *brigadiero* birthday treat!"

"I love it!" Stephanie shouted from the other room. "Save me one!"

This was truly going to be perfect and maybe our most international cupcake yet.

"Let's make a test batch, just in case," Em suggested.

I laughed, nodding. "Yes, chef!"

Thankfully, the recipe for this order was simple, so we already had all of the ingredients!

"Mom we're ready!" I called out. My mom rushed over from watching her late afternoon TV shows to set the oven to preheat and begin making the *brigadeiro* frosting.

To make *brigadeiros*, you have to put butter, condensed milk, and cocoa powder into a pot and stir it until nothing sticks to the pot. My mother had to stand over the stove while the rest of us made the batter. Teamwork makes the dream work!

Emily and I made the funfetti batter. Ethan and Ren were in charge of adding sprinkles into the batter as it mixed. And Alana set up the mini cupcake trays with cute cups that said "Happy Birthday!"

The test batch turned out great! We didn't have to wait long to taste test our creation since it was just the frosting that needed to cool in order to make it like a *brigadeiro*. Everyone was having the best time ever. Emily even laughed when she got some rainbow sprinkles in her sock. I was so excited for Helena to get these cupcakes for her party tomorrow.

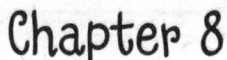

Chapter 8

Birthday Funday!

"Today's the big day!" my mom said, shutting off my alarm.

"What day? I live such an exciting life!" I joked.

As I was about to walk out of the house, Stephanie called out to me, "All ready to deliver the cupcakes to Helena's party?" She raised an eyebrow at me and smiled.

"Yep!" I exclaimed.

"Sounds great, and hey, don't forget to—"

But I knew what she was going to say.

"Save you one? Already did!"

When we all arrived at Helena's house to deliver her birthday cupcakes, I saw her out of the corner of my eye watching me. I smiled softly at her.

Helena started walking in my direction.

I had no idea what to say by the time she got in front of me.

"I hope you enjoy your cupcakes, Helena," I blurted.

She looked at me suspiciously. "Sure . . . let's just hope you didn't put anything gross in them since I wasn't being nice to you this week."

I shook my head. "I would never do that."

"If you say so . . ." Helena took a closer look at the cupcakes on the dessert table. "Hey, are these like *brigadeiros*?"

Helena said the word in a better Portuguese accent than I did. "Yeah, how did you know?"

Helena's tone of voice changed, and she sounded nicer. "Well, the rounded shape of them, the sprinkles all over, the gooey-looking chocolate topping . . . My mom is Brazilian and sometimes buys them at the Brazilian bakery as a special treat. We used to make them together with my grandmother . . ." For a second there as her voice trailed off, it looked like she got sad.

"That's so cool!" I said. "And I understand, grandmas are special."

"Yeah, her name was Helena too. By the way, the *H* in my name is silent. Portuguese is a lot like Spanish, no? Silent *H*?" Then Helena pronounced her name for me: "Ay-lane-ah."

"Ah, I didn't realize I've been mispronouncing it. It's important to say names right," I acknowledged.

"It's all good. Did you know it means shining light, my name? My parents told me they knew I'd shine brighter than the brightest star."

"You do," I replied.

"Yeah, I used to think so too. But when Ms. Geradi gave you the first solo part instead of me, I felt like I was disappearing. I didn't feel bright at all, and so I got jealous and was mean to you, Natalie. I'm really sorry."

"Thank you for apologizing," I said to Helena. "Luckily, there's enough room in the galaxy for all of us to shine bright! And life is a lot brighter with us all shining. Don't you think?"

"Totally," Helena agreed, and took a bite out of a *brigadeiro* mini cupcake. "Mmm, these are really good! Don't tell my mom or she'll be ordering them from you all the time!"

"Hey, that's not the worst thing that could happen," I joked.

Helena laughed. "That's true."

I smiled. "I'm glad we had this talk, Helena."

"Me too," she agreed.

"Okay, so tell me something. Am I pronouncing *brigadeiros* right?" I said, trying my best.

"*Bom trabalho!*" Helena replied in Portuguese.

"Good job?" I said cautiously. I wasn't sure if I was translating correctly.

"Exactly!" Helena replied, sounding proud of me.

"It sounds so similar to Spanish, but different, you know?"

Helena laughed. "Totally!"

Helena invited us all to stay and enjoy the party. We laughed and talked about food, culture, and language, and before we knew it, we both had forgotten about the week. I was happy I gave Helena a chance. Not everything or everyone is what it seems, but with a little kindness, patience, and delicious cupcakes, you can bring out the best in them.

Still Hungry?

Here's a bite of the seventh book in the Cupcake Diaries: The New Batch series, *Ren's Cupcake Mission*

"Time's up, class!"

Whew! I had just finished answering the last question on my history test with a few seconds to spare. *Two down, three to go,* I thought as I handed in my test and walked down the hallway for lunch.

Test-taking week at Fenton Street School was no joke. My whole grade was getting grilled on math, science, English, social studies, and gym. Yesterday, I had my gym exam—so easy! After history that morning, all I had left that day was my science test.

When I reached the cafeteria, I saw my friends Emily, Ethan, Natalie, and Alana sitting at our usual table. We're all part of the Mini Cupcake Club, and we normally bake treats for different events. But this week, we've all been studying hard for our tests. So that meant no baking.

"How was history?" asked Natalie as I sat down and took out my lunch.

"Not too hard," I replied. "You're taking the math test after lunch, right?"

Natalie nodded. "Stephanie helped me study." I was happy to hear that. Natalie and her twin sister, Stephanie, had recently gone through a rough patch, but they're a lot better now. It was awesome to hear that Stephanie was helping Natalie with her schoolwork. For a moment, I wished I had a sibling to help me study.

"I really miss baking," said Emily, biting into her sandwich.

"No orders for two weeks while we study. Grades matter," Alana reminded us.

"I know," Emily said with a sigh. "But I still miss it."

Before lunch ended, my friends and I promised to hop on a quick video call when we got home later to see how our latest tests went. I headed over to my next class, and before I knew it, the day was almost over, and it was time for my science exam.